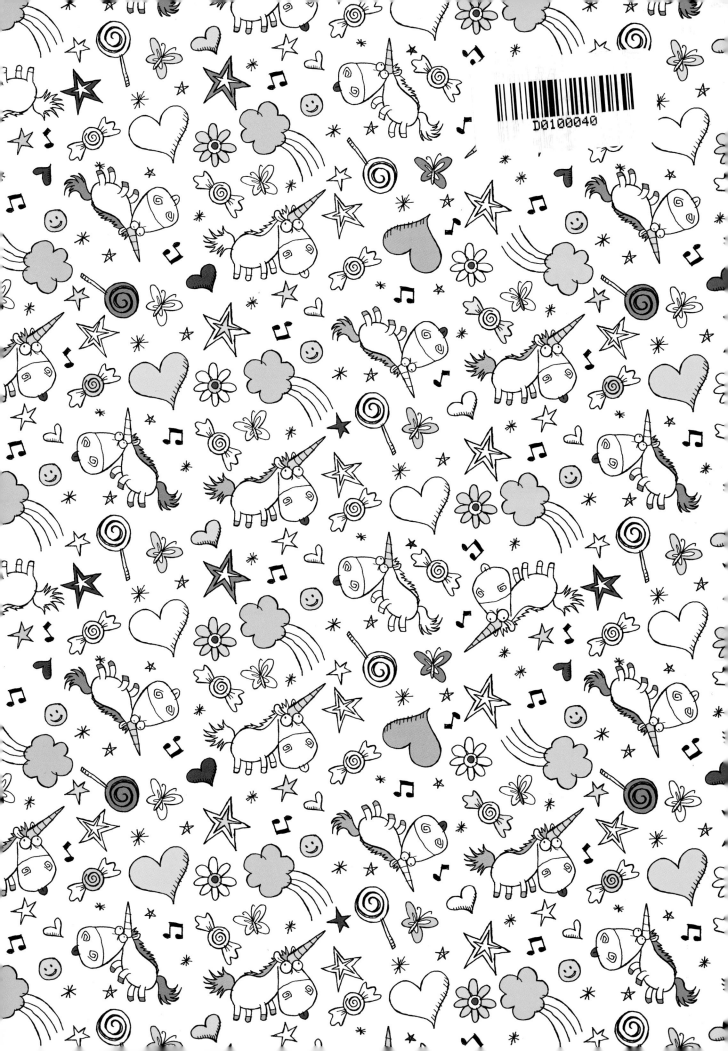

LITTLE, BROWN AND COMPANY
HACHETTE BOOK GROUP
1290 AVENUE OF THE AMERICAS, NEW YORK, NY 10104
VISIT US AT LB-KIDS.COM
WWW.DESPICABLE.ME

LITTLE, BROWN AND COMPANY IS A DIVISION OF HACHETTE BOOK GROUP, INC. THE LITTLE, BROWN NAME AND LOGO ARE TRADEMARKS OF HACHETTE BOOK GROUP, INC.

THE PUBLISHER IS NOT RESPONSIBLE FOR WEBSITES (OR THEIR CONTENT) THAT ARE NOT OWNED BY THE PUBLISHER.

PUBLISHED SIMULTANEOUSLY IN GREAT BRITAIN BY CENTRUM BOOKS LTD.
FIRST U.S. EDITION: MAY 2017

CENTRUM BOOKS LTD.
20 DEVON SQUARE
NEWTON ABBOT, DEVON, TQ12 2HR, UK
BOOKS@CENTRUMBOOKSLTD.CO.UK

ISBNS: 978-0-316-50747-9 (HARDCOVER), 978-0-316-50751-6 (EBOOK), 978-0-316-50748-6 (EBOOK), 978-0-316-50745-5 (EBOOK)

PRINTED IN THE UNITED STATES OF AMERICA

PHX

10 9 8 7 6 5 4 3 2 1

ILLUMINATION PRESENTS

DESPICABLE ME 3 ™

AGNES LOVES UNICORNS!

L B

LITTLE, BROWN AND COMPANY
New York Boston

Once upon a time, there was a little girl named AGNES. She had two older sisters—the oldest was named MARGO and the other was named EDITH. The three sisters were orphans and lived at Miss Hattie's Home for Girls.

Agnes
(THE YOUNGEST)

Margo
(THE OLDEST)

MISS HATTIE'S 😊
HOME FOR GIRLS

HOME for GIRLS

Edith
(THE MIDDLE SISTER)

Every night, when the girls went to sleep, AGNES DREAMED THAT A MOMMY AND DADDY WOULD ADOPT THEM. She was sure they would be adopted very soon and that the mommy and daddy would be nice. . . .

Margo, Edith, AND Agnes's ROOM IS HERE!

EDITH IS PRAYING THAT BUGS DON'T CRAWL INTO THEIR BRAINS. GROSS!

She also wanted a pet
UNICORN.

AGNES **LOVED**
UNICORNS. 🙂

She knew they were real. Every night she sang herself to
sleep with a song she had made up all about unicorns.

AGNES'S SONG

"Unicorns, I love them! Unicorns, I love them!

Uni, uni, unicorns, I lo-o-ove them!

Uni, unicorns, I could pet one, if they were

really real . . . and THEY ARE!

So, I bought one so I could pet it.

Now it loves me, now I love it!"

After she sang this, she always had the
MOST MAGICAL DREAMS all about unicorns.

ONE DAY, AGNES'S DREAM CAME TRUE...

just not exactly as she had always imagined.

Agnes and her sisters were adopted by Gru, who was a "dentist."

Gru (NOT A DENTIST)

THE GIRLS FIRST MEET GRU.

AGNES HAS GRU'S LEG. 😊

...ne day, Gru took the girls to **SUPER SILLY FUN LAND**—the most fun place ... Earth! It was here that Agnes first spotted something . . . **FLUFFY**.

It was **LOVE AT FIRST SIGHT!** The game they were playing was unfair, but luckily Gru had a gadget that helped level the playing field!

GRU'S GADGET THAT LEVELS THE PLAYING FIELD!

Agnes finally had a dad and her very own fluffy unicorn—perhaps the FLUFFIEST UNICORN EVER!

IT'S SO **FLUFFY**, I'M GONNA DIE!

SHE WAS SO HAPPY.

From that moment on, Agnes and Fluffy did **EVERYING** together.

FLUFFY IS **HERE!**

Tea parties with Gru, stories at bedtime. . .

ONE BIG UNICORN BY GRU

THIS STORY IS ABOUT UNICORNS, TOO!

...and board games with Margo. They also slept together side by side every night. Agnes **LOVED** Fluffy VERY MUCH.

One very scary time, when the Minion Kevin was injected with PX-41, PURPLE-KEVIN TRIED TO EAT FLUFFY! Agnes **SCREAMED** so loudly that all the windows and Kevin's goggles shattered. Kevin dropped Fluffy. Agnes saved the day!

KEVIN'S GOGGLES BEFOR THEY WERE BROKEN!

NO ONE CAN COME **BETWEEN** A GiRL
AND HER FLUFFY UNICORN!

As much as Agnes **LOVED** Fluffy, she loved
her family even more. So when her mommy
and daddy, Lucy and Gru, lost their jobs at
the AVL, Agnes knew what she had to do. She
held a yard sale to sell all her toys. . .

. . .INCLUDING HER BELOVED FLUFFY.

FLUFFY BEING SOLD. ☹

When the family went to visit Gru's newfound twin brother, Dru, in Freedonia, Agnes heard about a **LOCAL LEGEND.** The Legend stated that **REAL UNICORNS** roamed the nearby forest, and that if you were a maiden of the purest heart, you could find one.

AGNES AND EDITH EVEN FOUND A REAL UNICORN HORN IN A PUB! PROOF!

Agnes knew she had a PURE HEART, so she knew just what she had to do. . . .

Agnes and Edith set off into the forest, DETERMINED to find a MYSTICAL UNICORN. It would fulfill Agnes's lifelong dream to find and become friends with a unicorn, and Edith's more recent dream (in case unicorns did exist) of filming a unicorn and selling the video to become rich.

THIS IS HOW EDITH FEELS ABOUT THE QUEST.

THIS IS HOW EDITH IMAGINES SHE'LL FEEL IF UNICORNS ARE REAL AND SHE FILMS IT.

WHEN AGNES FINDS A UNICORN, SHE WILL GIVE IT THE BIGGEST HUG!

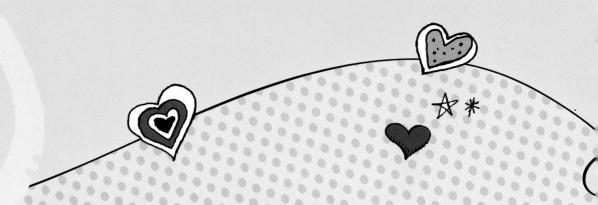

In the end, the maiden with the purest heart found something that she knew was a unicorn in the forest.

AND IT WAS LOVE AT FIRST SIGHT.

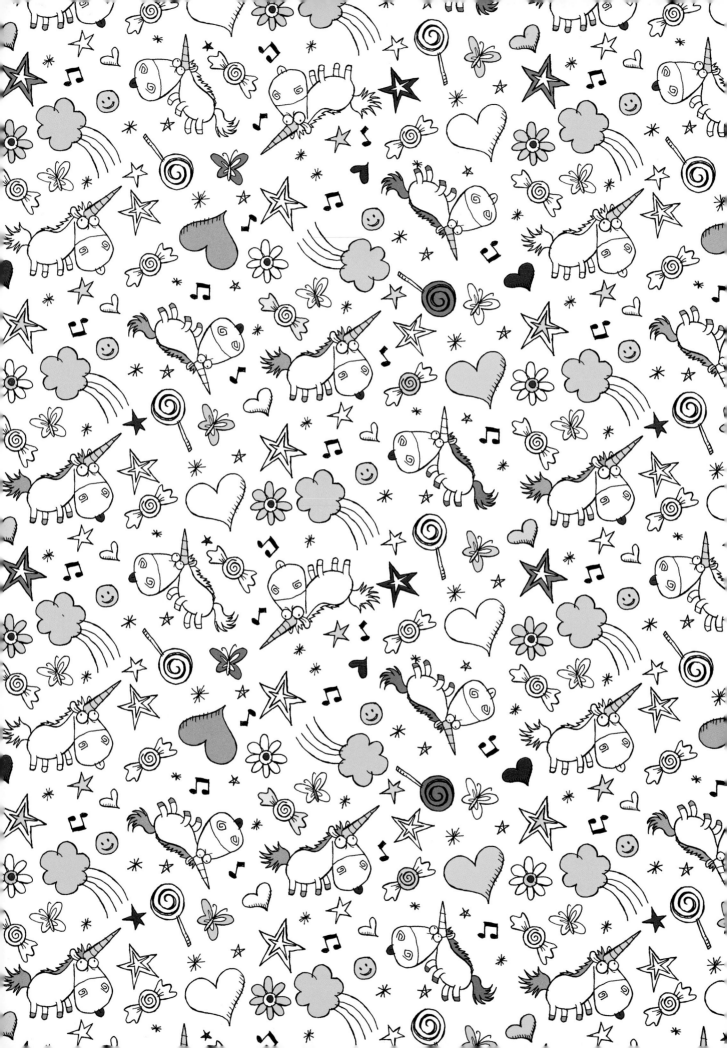